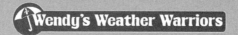

Sno-vember!

by **Kathryn Lay**   illustrated by **Jason Wolff**

visit us at www.abdopublishing.com

To the Stuards, a friendship stronger than any storm— KL

Published by Magic Wagon, a division of the ABDO Group,
8000 West 78th Street, Edina, Minnesota 55439. Copyright
© 2011 by Abdo Consulting Group, Inc. International copyrights
reserved in all countries. All rights reserved. No part of this book
may be reproduced in any form without written permission from
the publisher.

Calico Chapter Books™ is a trademark and logo of Magic Wagon.

Printed in the United States of America, Melrose Park, Illinois.
032010
092010

 This book contains at least 10% recycled materials.

Text by Kathryn Lay
Illustrations by Jason Wolff
Edited by Stephanie Hedlund and Rochelle Baltzer
Cover and interior design by Abbey Fitzgerald

Library of Congress Cataloging-in-Publication Data
Lay, Kathryn.
  Sno-vember! / by Kathryn Lay ; illustrated by Jason Wolff.
     p. cm. -- (Wendy's weather warriors ; bk. 3)
  Includes bibliographical references and index.
  ISBN 978-1-60270-756-6 (alk. paper)
  1. Snow--Juvenile literature. I. Wolff, Jason, ill. II. Title.
  QC926.37.L39 2010
  551.57'84--dc22
                              2009048836

CONTENTS

CHAPTER 1

A Contest

"Gobble, gobble, gobble!"

Austin Scott ran past Wendy Peters and grabbed the notebook out of her hand.

"Hey, give that back!" she shouted.

Austin dodged around the desks, gobbling and holding up Wendy's notebook. He ran around until Dennis Galloway grabbed it.

"Gobble!" Austin said one last time.

Wendy took the notebook from Dennis. "I'll be glad when Thanksgiving is over and Austin quits gobbling," she said. She opened the deep blue notebook. She had glued paper snowflakes on the cover.

"I'm glad it snows here. Where we used to live, it hardly ever snowed. I can't wait! I want enough snow to throw snowballs and build a snow fort."

Jessica Roberts nodded. "It's so pretty. I've got some great snow pictures."

Dennis shrugged. "It's not even Thanksgiving yet. We don't usually get snow until closer to Christmas. Sometimes not until January."

He tapped the small notebook in his shirt pocket. Wendy knew he was thinking about snow experiments.

Wendy tapped her folder. "I've learned all about snow. Did you know that snow is a mineral? Like diamonds. Or salt."

Katie Carter shook her head until her curls bounced. "My mom just got diamond earrings. I don't think she'd like snow earrings."

Austin shouted, "Can I put snow on top of my popcorn?" He pretended to munch on popcorn.

Wendy sighed. "I don't mean that snow is really like diamonds or popcorn."

Mr. Andrews tapped his ruler on his head. That meant to be quiet and sit down. When everyone was sitting, Mr. Andrews said, "I know everyone is ready for the Thanksgiving break. But before the bell rings, I have an exciting announcement from Mrs. Stuard."

Wendy leaned forward. Mrs. Stuard was the best principal anyone ever had.

Mr. Andrews walked up and down the aisles. "There will be a snowman-building contest at the first snow this year," he explained. "Next summer a new water park opens. They are donating four tickets to the winners of each class."

Wendy heard gasps around her. She had heard about Splash World opening that summer. It was going to have corkscrew waterslides and a wave pool.

Kevin Gray raised his hand. "What if it snows on the weekend and not on a school day?"

"The contest will happen on the first day there is snow on the school grounds on a school day," Mr. Andrews said. "But I wouldn't expect any snow for several more weeks, maybe not until after the Christmas break even."

Wendy raised her hand. "It's got to be more than just cold in the air around us to have snow. The air has to be cold all the way up a couple miles for snow. There can't be any warm air above us. Could we keep a class log with weather information in it every day?"

"Good idea, Wendy," Mr. Andrews said. "We can't make it snow, but we can learn a lot about what has to happen before it will snow."

Dennis raised his hand. "Mr. Andrews, you're wrong. I know how we can make snow."

He stood up and cleared his throat. Wendy grinned at Jessica. If anyone knew how to make snow, it would be Dennis.

"You can make pretend snow with instant mashed potato flakes or soap flakes or pieces of paper cut up or . . . "

Austin jumped out of his chair. "If we make mashed potato snowmen, we could have a snowman-eating contest. How do you make snow gravy?"

Everyone laughed. Dennis glared at Austin and sat down.

Mr. Andrews tapped the ruler on his head again. "Dennis, those are all interesting ideas for making a small amount of pretend snow. I'm afraid it would be hard to build snowmen out of them. However, they would be fun projects for a snow lesson."

Dennis nodded. Wendy had to admit that Mr. Andrews was right. How could you build a snowman with soap flakes?

The bell rang and everyone grabbed their backpacks.

"Yeah!" Jessica shouted.

Wendy and Jessica walked out the door together.

"Let's have a Weather Warriors meeting the day after Thanksgiving," Wendy said. "Tomorrow the school choir is singing at the homeless shelter. We're doing a special Thanksgiving program for the kids."

"Wow," Jessica said. "I bet that would make a great picture!"

"So, should we meet on Friday in the clubhouse?" Wendy asked.

Jessica got in line to wait for her mother to pick her up. "You bet. I can't wait to show you and Dennis my new camera. I bought it when I sold the lightning picture to the newspaper."

Dennis poked his head between them. "Cool. And you know what else is cool? Snow cones and snow forts and sledding."

Austin walked past them on his way to the bus. "You three think you know everything about snow. But I know something, too. I know how to cover the school grounds with snow."

"Sure you do," Wendy said, rolling her eyes at Jessica.

Austin stuck his tongue at them. "My dad is buying a snow-making machine. I'm going to practice building snowmen in my backyard and I'll win those tickets to the water park."

CHAPTER 2

A Good Idea and a Bad One

The day after Thanksgiving, Wendy sat in the weather clubhouse with Dennis and Jessica. They were eating leftover pumpkin pie with lots of whipped cream on top.

"Hey, how about whipped-cream snow?" Dennis suggested.

"You can't make a snowman out of whipped cream," Jessica said with a giggle.

Wendy held out her snow notebook. "I don't want whipped-cream snow or potato-flake snow. I want snow that you can roll into balls and sled across. And, I want to win that snowman-building contest."

Dennis nodded. "Me too. I went to a water park once on vacation. I was only four and I had to stay in the kid pool and float on the lazy river."

Something scratched at the clubhouse door. Dennis jumped up and opened it. A little burst of curly-haired energy ran into the room. Jessica giggled when Cumulus licked her hand where she'd dipped her fingers into the whipped cream.

"I bet Cumulus would have fun in the snow," Jessica said. She grabbed her backpack and carefully pulled out a camera bag. "Here's my new camera. It has an extra lens for taking real close shots of things."

She pulled out a long lens and attached it to the camera, then pointed it at Cumulus.

Dennis reached over and wiped a big glob of whipped cream on the Schnoodle's nose.

"Great shot!" Jessica said as she snapped the picture. She pointed at the digital screen. "Look, Cumulus's nose looks like a shiny black mountain with snow on top."

Wendy picked up a small pumpkin sitting beside her ham radio. "The choir did the special show at the homeless shelter on Wednesday. It was a little scary at first, but then it was fun. The kids clapped and gave us hugs. I hope we go back for Christmas."

"Cool," Dennis mumbled, chewing the last bite of his pie. "But what about the snow? I wonder if Austin's dad is really putting together a snow machine."

"Austin talked like it was real," Wendy said.

"I'd sure like to see it," Dennis said. "It's something a weather scientist like me would love."

Wendy snapped her fingers. "We could go over to Austin's house and see if his Dad is really building a snow machine."

Dennis jumped up. "Why didn't I think of that?"

"We'll go tomorrow," Wendy said.

Could Austin really make his own snow? Wendy just had to find a way to talk him into letting them play in it, too. She had another idea, but she didn't think the other Weather Warriors would like it.

In fact, she *knew* they wouldn't like it at all.

CHAPTER 3

A Mad Scientist Makes Snow

Wendy looked out the window at her front door for the tenth time that Saturday morning. On the eleventh time, she saw Dennis and Jessica standing on her porch.

"My mom said she'd drive us to Austin's house. Does anyone know where Austin lives?" Wendy said.

Dennis pulled out his notebook. "I wrote it down here. Austin used to be in my Boy Scout troop and we had a meeting at his house once."

"Isn't he in Boy Scouts anymore?" Jessica asked. She slung her camera bag over her shoulder.

"He said it was boring and he quit," Dennis said. He leaned closer and whispered, "But I think he got into trouble on a field trip to a farm. He opened the gate and let the bull out!"

Wendy's mother jingled her car keys. "Okay, let's get going. Are you sure it's okay for you to just pop over to their house? His parents may have other plans."

"It's not very far away, Mrs. Peters," Dennis said. "If they're busy, we could just come back to the clubhouse."

"Please, Mom?" Wendy asked. She hoped Austin's parents weren't busy. She wanted to see a snow machine. And she wanted to know if the snow it made felt and looked like real snow.

It was a short drive to Austin's house. Wendy's mother waited with them at the front door. They waited and waited after Wendy rang the bell.

"Oh my, Austin didn't say he was having friends over," Mrs. Scott said when she opened the door. Her hands were covered in muddy-looking clay.

"Sorry to just show up," Wendy's mother said. "The kids heard about your husband's snow machine."

Mrs. Scott smiled. "Oh yes, Austin and his father are in the garage. Let me wipe this clay off my hands and I'll show you."

They followed Mrs. Scott to the kitchen. "I was just finishing up a new vase design when the doorbell rang."

"Do you make pottery?" Wendy asked.

"Yes, I guess I've been doing it since before Austin was born." She pointed toward the kitchen. "If you go out that back door, you'll find Austin in the garage. They've been working for a while, so they might be nearly done."

Wendy's mother said, "Call me when you're done and I'll come pick you up."

Wendy nodded and grabbed Jessica's arm. Dennis followed them out the back door and into a side door of the garage. They were just in time to see Austin's dad wearing goggles and tightening a bolt on a green machine. It looked like it was part lawnmower and part vacuum cleaner. It had small wheels and a long hose.

"That is amazing," Dennis whispered.

"I think we're done," Mr. Scott said. He stood up and plugged it in. The machine sputtered and shook a moment, then roared to life. It reminded Wendy of the generator her father had in case a storm knocked out their electricity.

Austin rubbed his hands together like a mad scientist. "I want snow!" And with that, he flipped a switch.

Mr. Scott leaped forward and shouted, "No, not in here!"

Wendy gasped as jets of snow flew upward, falling down on her head. The snow came faster and faster. Soon, it covered the car, the tools, and even the washer and dryer as Austin sprayed everything in sight.

CHAPTER 4

Wendy's Warriors Plus One

Austin's dad grabbed the switch and flipped it off. As fast as it had started, the machine stopped. The last bits of cold snow floated around the garage.

"Son, we need to move this into the backyard before we turn it on," Austin's father explained patiently. He suddenly seemed to notice the others. "Well, if it isn't our heroes."

Austin snorted. "Heroes? You mean weirdos."

His father gave Austin a nudge. "I mean heroes. If they hadn't stopped us that day at the big game, we might have been hit by the lightning that struck that van."

Dennis ran his hand over the machine. He bent down and looked at it from every side. "Austin told us about your snow machine, and we just had to see it."

Jessica snapped a quick photo of the machine and another of the snow on the dryer.

"I hardly ever saw snow where I used to live," Wendy explained.

Austin's father said, "Well then, let's get this into the backyard and see what we can do."

Wendy and her friends helped him carry the machine through the garage and back gate.

"Wow, what a great backyard!" Dennis said.

The end of the yard sloped down into a hill. In one corner of the yard, there was a corkscrew slide, a picnic table, and chairs with thick cushions.

Mr. Scott pointed the hose of the snow-making machine at the middle of the yard. "Alright, give me a countdown."

"Ten, nine, eight . . . ," they shouted.

Austin yelled louder and louder. When they got to three, two, one, Wendy was holding her ears.

Mr. Scott nodded to Austin, who flipped the switch again.

Snow shot out of the hose. When snow covered an area, Austin's father moved the machine. Soon, the slide, picnic table, and every bit of the hill had snow.

When he stopped, it looked like a winter blizzard had hit Austin's backyard. Wendy was glad it was a cold afternoon so the snow wouldn't melt too quickly.

"Okay, kids. Have fun," Mr. Scott said. He brushed some snow off one of the chairs and sat down.

Austin grabbed a trash can lid off the porch and shouted, "Wahooooo!" He leaped onto it and slid down the hill.

Wendy bent over and touched the snow. It was cold and clumped in her hand. She tried rolling it into a small ball, like a snow cone. Would it hold together? She tossed it straight at Dennis's back.

"Hey!" he shouted, grabbing a handful to toss back at her.

Before Wendy could shout "snowball fight," soggy snowballs were flying.

They stopped, out of breath, as Austin trudged back up the hill. Wendy got him with a snowball right on top of his head. He patted it onto his hair.

The kids slid down the snow-covered slide and took turns zipping down the hill on the trash can lid.

"Let's practice building snowmen," Dennis suggested.

Jessica was already half done with one.

"It's lopsided," Dennis said, turning his head. "I don't think that would win Mrs. Stuard's contest."

Wendy snapped her fingers. The contest! "You know, if we came over here every day, we could practice building the best snowmen in school," she said.

Dennis stuffed a snowy head on his melting snowman body. "Hey, Austin, can we?"

Austin kicked at his own snowman until it crumbled into a snowy pile. "Why should I?"

Wendy took a deep breath. It was time for her bad idea, the one she knew her friends wouldn't like. "What if we made you an honorary member of the Weather Warriors?"

Austin's eyes went wide. "I could come to your clubhouse?"

Jessica had just focused her camera to take a picture of a blue jay sitting on the snowy slide. She jumped, scaring away the bird. "What?" she shouted.

Wendy wanted to change her mind. Then she thought about the contest and about winning the tickets to the water park. And most of all, she thought about getting to play in snow every day.

Before she could change her mind she held out her hand and said, "Deal!"

CHAPTER 5

Dandruff and Other Types of Snow

On Monday morning, the first person Wendy saw when she walked into Circleville Elementary was Austin.

"So, when is the next club meeting?" Austin asked as he bounced up and down like a kangaroo.

"I'm not sure," Wendy mumbled. "Maybe after school today . . . or maybe tomorrow."

"Great. After the meeting, you can come to my house and play in the snow in my backyard," Austin said.

"Snow?" a kid asked, nudging his friends. "We haven't had any snow yet."

Wendy grabbed Austin by the arm and led him to class. "Listen, you can't let everyone know about your snow. We can practice and be the best snowman builders in the school by the time real snow comes."

Austin nodded. "And whoever wins the four tickets will take the other three to the water park. Right? Okay? We're all in this together. Our secret."

Wendy agreed. It was their secret. She wondered what the other kids would say if they knew. It wasn't really cheating, was it?

They were the last ones to find their seats in class.

Jessica leaned across her desk and whispered, "I can't believe you said Austin could join our club."

Wendy shrugged. "What could I do? You want to win those tickets, don't you? He said we could come over again."

"Today after school?" Jessica asked.

Wendy shook her head and stared at her desk. "Uh, no. After the Weather Warriors meeting."

Jessica frowned.

Mr. Andrews walked to the back of the room. He pulled out a large hamster from a cage and put it on his shoulder.

"Wow, Mr. Andrews. Did you give Sneakers super-grow food during the break?" Debbie Saunders asked.

Mr. Andrews smiled. "He has gotten a little chubby, hasn't he? But, he's all ready for winter."

Sarah Perkins raised her hand. "Can we talk about the snowman contest?"

"Mrs. Stuard will make an announcement about it soon," Mr. Andrews explained. "But for now, we have work to do. Wendy had a good idea to keep records of the temperatures. We'll also chart the cloud formations every day."

Dennis's hand shot up. "Which freezes faster, cold water or warm? Just get me a couple of cups of water and . . . "

Mr. Andrews interrupted. "Good idea, Dennis. We'll do some cold weather experiments. According to weather reports, we're expected to have colder than normal temperatures this week."

Austin waved both his arms. "Yeah, especially in my backyard."

Wendy groaned. Austin was going to spill the beans and then everyone would want to practice snowman building.

Wendy blurted out, "Did you know that a man named Wilson Bentley took more than 5,000 pictures of snowflakes through his microscope? He was the one who proved that every snowflake is different."

Jessica squealed. "Five thousand pictures? That's amazing."

Mr. Andrews cleared his throat.

"Wendy, that's very interesting," he said, "but please raise your hand first next time."

Wendy raised her hand and waited for Mr. Andrews to point at her. "I have a whole notebook about snow. Did you know that snowflakes are made of dust?"

Austin snorted. "They are not. They're made of cold stuff."

Mr. Andrews leaned against his desk and let Sneakers crawl down his arm into his empty coffee cup. "Actually, Wendy is partially correct. Snowflakes begin as water vapor, ice crystals, and dust. The water vapor freezes on the dust to create ice crystals."

"You mean like the dust on my mom's lighthouse collection?" Gabe Sanchez asked. "Those things are really dusty."

Wendy shook her head. "No, like dust from flower pollen or even volcanoes or meteorites."

Austin's eyes got wide. Mr. Andrews smiled. "Yes," he said. "And when clouds have both extremely cold water droplets and ice crystals, snow will start to form.

"As the snowflakes form and fall through the cloud, they go through other clouds. When the ice crystals stick together and the clouds they pass through have different temperatures, the flake changes shape and size.

"What's important is that all temperatures at the different levels have to be below freezing," ended Mr. Andrews.

Wendy held up her snow notebook. She opened it to a page and read, "There are seven types of ice crystal shapes. They are called Stellar (which is star shaped), plates, columns, capped columns, needle, spatial dendrite, and irregular crystal."

Austin laughed. "One is called Special Dandruff?"

Everyone else laughed. Wendy couldn't help but giggle. It did sound weird.

Mr. Andrews slipped Sneakers back into his cage. "Let's move on to math. We'll talk more about the cold temperatures and what needs to happen for snow during science."

Wendy covered her mouth with her hand. She knew what had to happen for it to snow. But she also knew a secret that only three other kids in class knew.

There was going to be snow at Austin's house that night.

CHAPTER 6

Practice Makes Perfect

Austin ran from one part of the clubhouse to another. He grabbed the ham radio microphone and shouted, "Anybody out there?"

Wendy pulled it from his hand. "I'm the only one who uses the ham," she said.

"What's this?" Austin asked. He stared into the rain gauge Wendy had brought in for the winter. Then, he held it up and said, "Aargh, I'm a pirate and here be me spyglass."

"He's going to break something," Jessica said. She held on tightly to her camera bag.

Dennis followed Austin and explained everything to him until Wendy said, "That's enough for tonight, Austin. We need to have a quick meeting and go to your house to build . . . "

"Snowmen!" Austin shouted. "Slushy, mushy, giant snowmen!"

Everyone sat around the card table in the middle of the clubhouse. Then Wendy said, "If we're going to win this contest, we have to keep quiet about Austin's snow machine or everyone will want to come."

"My backyard isn't big enough for everyone at school," Austin said.

"Well, it's our secret," Wendy said. "And if you want to be a Weather Warrior, you have to keep quiet about it."

Austin put his fingers to his lips and nodded.

Wendy held out a sheet of paper. "I got the secretary to make me a copy of the flyer for the contest. It says we can use anything we want to make our snowman. You know, for its face or clothes."

She passed the paper around. "So we need to come up with our own ideas for the best-looking snowman," she said, waving another piece of paper. "I found this online. It's the biggest snowman EVER."

Everyone crowded together to read the information.

> "The world's largest snowman was named Angus and was built in Bethel, Maine, in 1999. He was 113 feet and 7 inches tall. Angus was made of 9,000,000 pounds of snow, two 4-foot wreathes as eyes, 6 feet of chicken wire and muslin for the

nose, six automobile tires as the mouth, a 20-foot fleece hat, a 120-foot fleece scarf, three more tires for the buttons and two 10-foot trees for the arms."

Dennis whistled. "Wow, I'd like to have seen that."

Austin jumped up. "Come on, let's go build a snowman. I've got lots of junk in my garage."

Wendy's mother drove them to Austin's house. They burst inside and surrounded Mr. Scott.

"Is there snow yet?"

Austin's father laughed. "Yes, I just finished a few minutes ago. If it melts, come tell me. I don't want anyone tampering with the machine without me."

He was barely done talking before they were running to the back door.

"It looks even more amazing than last time," Wendy said. She scooped up a handful of snow and rubbed it in Dennis's hair. He shook it off and chased her up the slide and down it again.

Jessica took pictures of the yard and close-up shots of a snow-covered pink flamingo.

"Come on, we can't waste time," Wendy said. "Mom said I have to be home in an hour."

They scooped and rolled the snow into snowmen. Then they searched for new ideas to make the snowmen look exciting.

Dennis put an oil funnel on his for a nose.

Austin stuck a beat-up straw hat on his and covered the snowman's chest with buttons from a can.

Jessica found some old plastic flowers and stuck them on her snowman's head. "Look, he's blooming hair!"

Wendy rolled two flat tires into the backyard and covered them with snow. Her snowman looked wider than the others.

"Hey," Jessica said. "What'll we do about having this stuff at school? We might not know when it's going to snow."

Wendy folded her arms. "I think we have to use stuff we can find around the school. Like rulers or sticks on the ground."

Jessica took pictures of each of their snowmen.

"Just in case we aren't prepared for the first real snow," she said.

"We'll be ready," Wendy said. "We're the Weather Warriors."

They all gave a shout while Austin ran around his snowman yelling, "I'm a Weather Warrior, too!"

CHAPTER 7

Reading the Signs

"When will it snow, Mr. Andrews?" Joey Peterson asked.

Mr. Andrews sighed. "I know everyone is excited about the snowman contest, but we can't spend every day in class worrying about when it will snow."

"Can we check today's temperature?" Wendy asked.

Mr. Andrews nodded. He picked up the special giant weather thermometer that he'd brought to class. Everyone grabbed their coats off the hooks at the back of class, lined up, and followed him out the classroom door. They walked down the hall and outside to the school garden, where Circleville students planted and weeded once a week.

Mr. Andrews set the thermometer on the picnic table in the center of the garden area. Everyone crowded around.

Wendy had her snow notebook to record the temperature. When they got back to class, she would put it on the poster they had made for the classroom.

"Hey, look at those clouds!" Austin shouted, jumping up and grabbing at the air as if he could pull down the clouds. "Those look like snow clouds to me."

Before Wendy could tell him how silly he was, Dennis shook his head. "Those are just cirrus clouds. You need Nimbostratus clouds before there's a chance of snow."

Mr. Andrews nodded. "Yes, but what if we get lots of wind? Will that affect the possibility of snow?"

Wendy smiled. She opened her notebook and read a moment. Then she said, "If we get strong winds going from northeast to southwest, we could have snow."

"Okay," Mr. Andrews said. "Someone tell me what the thermometer reads and what time it is now."

Austin put his face up against the thermometer. "I don't hear it reading."

Jessica laughed. Austin crossed his eyes at her.

Dale Nations said, "My watch says 9:47. And the thermometer is at 35 degrees."

"Below 32 degrees is freezing," Wendy said. "We're almost there."

Mr. Andrews picked up the thermometer and moved everyone back in line. "That's true, but I'd be surprised to see any snow this soon. It's still November."

As they walked back to class, Wendy whispered to Jessica and Dennis, "Dad told me this morning that his meteorologist friend at the news station believes we'll have snow sooner than everyone thinks."

"Today?" Jessica asked. "I've got my camera batteries all charged for the snowman contest."

Wendy shook her head. "Not today, but soon."

Back at her desk, she wrote a quick note and dropped it on Austin's desk.

Austin, can we come practice building snowmen after school?

She watched him while he read it. He looked at her and moved his head up and down like a bobble doll. She figured that meant *Yes*.

Wendy would tell Dennis and Jessica during lunch. She didn't know how much more practice time they'd have before it snowed. If anyone should win those tickets, it should be the Weather Warriors.

They just had to win.

CHAPTER 8

Snow ... Snow ... Gone!

"I think today is the day," Wendy told everyone in Mr. Andrews's class the next morning.

"What day?" Dana Breedlove asked.

"Our first day of snow," Wendy said.

Dana looked out the window. "You're crazy. It's still November. We just had Thanksgiving last week. Last year it didn't snow until almost Christmas."

Wendy walked to the window. "Look, those are cumulus clouds. And the wind is picking up. This morning, I saw that the temperature had dropped to 33 degrees. It's almost freezing."

Everyone jumped out of their seats and ran to the window.

"I don't see any snow," Austin said. He turned and whispered, "But I know where you can find some."

Wendy put her fingers to her lips. How would she ever keep Austin from telling?

Mr. Andrews moved to the window. "Wendy is right, though. Everything points to snow today, but the meteorologist I heard this morning wasn't expecting us to get much. It may not even cover the ground."

"Then we couldn't have a snowman-building contest," Kevin Gray said.

Mr. Andrews swept his arms toward the desks. "For now, we need to get back to schoolwork. I know this is on your minds, but it's on my mind that we need to prepare for tomorrow's math test."

Wendy followed the rest of the class back to their seats. Who wanted to think about math tests when it might snow?

She tried to concentrate on what Mr. Andrews was saying about fractions. When he called her to the board to work on a problem, she forgot how to multiply two fractions with the same denominator.

Austin pointed and laughed when she got the wrong answer. Wendy glared at him. Why had she let him join the Weather Warriors? Why did he want to? He didn't even care about weather, especially not like her and her friends.

Mr. Andrews said, "Okay, Austin. Why don't you show us how to do it correctly?"

Wendy erased her answers and watched while Austin worked on the math problem. She could tell he really was trying, but he couldn't get it right either.

Maybe Mr. Andrews was right, they needed more practice.

When the lunch bell rang, Wendy grabbed her lunch box and ran to catch up with Jessica.

"What will we do if there's not enough snow to build a snowman?" Jessica asked.

Wendy sighed as they found their seats in the cafetorium. "I don't know. Guess we'll have to wait until the next snow."

Dennis sat across from them. "But the rules say 'the first snow.' Mrs. Stuard likes to follow rules."

"Wow, cool. Here it comes," someone said.

Wendy turned her head when several kids started to shout, "Snow! It's really snowing."

Outside the windows that lined one side of the cafetorium, Wendy could see the white flakes drifting down. While she watched, they came faster and faster.

There were more shouts in the cafetorium, and then everyone started talking. They got out of the lunch line, they got up from their seats, and they left their lunches to run to the windows.

Wendy stared at the snow, imagining each flake different from the next.

Dennis stood beside her. "I have an experiment where we can get a close look at the snowflakes."

Wendy grinned. Dennis had an experiment for everything.

"Excuse me, everyone please go back to their lunches," a voice said.

Wendy turned from the window to the stage. There, Mrs. Stuard was holding a microphone.

"The snow will keep for a while. Please finish your lunches and return to your classes. We'll end classes thirty minutes early today for you to build your snowmen. After twenty minutes, Mr. Rodriguez and I will judge them. We'll announce the winners tomorrow morning."

Wendy could feel her heart pounding. The principal and vice principal would have lots of snowmen to look at. She knew that everyone wanted to win those tickets. But no one else got to practice before the snow came. No one except her, Dennis, Jessica, and Austin.

Back in class, Mr. Andrews said, "Once again, Wendy proves that she knows her weather facts. It did snow today!"

Wendy grinned as everyone cheered. She turned to watch the beautiful snowflakes coming down. But there wasn't any snow to watch.

"Oh no!" she shouted. "It's not snowing anymore."

She could see that the ground had snow on it, but it was such a small amount she could see the grass underneath.

"I'm sorry," Mr. Andrews said. "We're lucky to have any snow this time of year."

The intercom crackled and Mrs. Stuard announced, "As many of you have probably noticed, the snow has stopped. The weather reports don't predict any more snow today or this week.

"It would be impossible to build large snowmen out of what we have outside, but I know you are all excited about the first snow. So, we will have a mini-snowman contest. For everyone who participates, I will get your name from your teachers and draw for the free passes to the water park."

Wendy frowned. There would be no snowmen built with tire tummies. There wasn't even enough snow to build one big enough to stick in a carrot for a nose.

She looked at Austin. He crossed his eyes at her. Then he grinned. He made a motion with his hand like someone flipping a switch. Then he waved his arms and made a whooshing noise.

Wendy's eyes went wide. She snapped her fingers. Austin had an idea. A *great* idea.

And Wendy's Weather Warriors were going to help him.

CHAPTER 9

Teeny, Tiny Snowmen

The school yard was crowded with kids standing in front of small piles of snow. They had scraped snow from the grass, the bushes, the sidewalk, and the playground equipment. Some of the teachers had taken containers from the cafeteria to get snow from their cars.

"On your mark, get set, go!" Mrs. Stuard shouted.

Wendy knelt down on the ground to build her miniature snowman.

"This is harder than building a regular-sized one," Jessica said.

Wendy agreed. She rolled and patted the snow into three small snowballs, each one bigger than the last. She took some raisins leftover from her lunch and made eyes. Then she took a broken orange crayon for the nose. More raisins made the smile. She used tiny twigs from under a tree to make arms.

"Well, that's kind of boring," Wendy said. She looked around. There was a sea of tiny snowmen, but most didn't even have faces at all. Some only had eyes.

"I made a Cyclops snowman!" Austin shouted.

A round cookie was the only thing in the middle of his snowman's face.

Dennis said, "We could've used this snow for experiments instead. All we need to do is scoop up some snow and take it to a microwave. I bet there's one in the teacher's lounge. Then we . . . "

Austin folded his arms. "I want super-sized snowmen. I want sneaky snowball fights. I want a snow fort."

He grabbed Wendy's sleeve and said, "Come on."

She jumped up and followed him to where Mrs. Stuard and Mr. Rodriguez were bending down to study a pair of snowmen twins. They were as long as a ruler, bigger than most of the other snowmen.

Austin jumped around and shouted, "Mrs. Stuard! Mrs. Stuard! Guess what my dad bought." His foot smashed down right on top of one of the snow twins.

"Hey, look what you did!" Marshall Henderson shouted.

Austin looked down at the smashed snowman. "Oops, sorry."

Mrs. Stuard motioned Austin and Wendy to move away from the other snowmen. "Calm down, Austin. Did you build a snowman? We'll get to it, I promise."

Wendy shook her head. "That's not what he wants to tell you. Is it, Austin?"

Austin grinned. "Nope. I can make snow."

Mrs. Stuard smiled and winked at Wendy.

"Really, Mrs. Stuard. He can," Wendy said. "But not with clouds and cold temperatures and dust and—"

Austin put his hand over Wendy's mouth. He told the principal about the weather machine his father built and how his backyard had become a snow park.

"We could bring it to the school and have a *real* snowman contest. And snowball fights and snow forts and . . ."

Mrs. Stuard tapped her finger against her chin. "That's very nice of you, Austin."

Wendy agreed. She still didn't know if Austin was a real Weather Warrior, but for now, he was an honorary one. And he was being nicer than she had been when she tried to hide their snowman practice.

Mrs. Stuard pointed to the melting miniature snowmen. "I don't know how to choose winners for the contest with this. Your snow machine wouldn't be real snow. But I don't want to just turn away those free tickets. Someone should get to use them."

Wendy snapped her fingers. She had an idea.

But would everyone at Circleville Elementary give up the chance to get free tickets to the water park?

CHAPTER 10

Two Great Ideas

Wendy whispered her plan to Mrs. Stuard. "That's a wonderful idea," the principal said. "And I think I have a way we can convince everyone else to agree."

She whispered her own great idea to Wendy. Wendy ran straight to Jessica and told her their plans.

After school, Wendy's father drove Wendy, Dennis, Jessica, and Austin to the city's homeless shelter. Dennis's parents came too and helped the Weather Warriors with their new project.

At school the next day, there was a special assembly called after morning roll.

"What's going on?" Dana asked.

Wendy just smiled. In all the school, no one but the principal and the Weather Warriors knew.

In the cafetorium, the projector screen had been lowered on the stage.

"Hey, we're going to watch a movie," Austin announced.

Wendy nudged him. He looked at her and said, "Oh yeah, I almost forgot."

Mr. Andrews said, "Not a movie, but something special."

Wendy looked at him and he winked. She grinned back. Mrs. Stuard must have told the teachers about the Warriors' idea.

The lights dimmed and the first of Jessica's pictures came on the screen.

A group of kids stood together, smiling at the camera and waving. Behind them, long rows of cots were lined up in a large room. The next photo showed several kids sitting on the cots. Some were holding stuffed animals and worn-out dolls.

The room got quiet as more pictures flashed by. There were pictures of families eating together on long tables and of adults standing in line to get food. There was also a picture of an older kid playing a guitar all alone in a corner.

Mrs. Stuard moved to the microphone and said, "These photos are of families who live at the Circleville Homeless Shelter. The parents are looking for jobs and hope to someday move into their own homes. But for now, these kids spend much of their time here. Some of our students have an idea we hope you will go along with."

Wendy and the Warriors jumped up and walked to the stage.

"The snow we had yesterday was great. It was also pretty small. We were all hoping for an early snow, but it doesn't look like we'll have another one for a while. The Weather Warriors have an idea. A snowy idea," Wendy said.

Dennis took the microphone. "Thanks to Austin Scott, we're going to have the biggest, best snow party ever! His dad's snow machine will make enough snow for snowball fights and snow games and more great stuff."

Jessica took the microphone from Dennis. "I'm going to take pictures of everything and we'll hang them in the halls. We'll even have a cardboard snowman where you can put your face through a cutout and have your picture taken."

Austin shouted, "My turn, my turn!"

He put the microphone right against his mouth. He howled like a dog and the speakers let out crackling static.

Mrs. Stuard stepped toward him. "Austin, move the microphone farther from your mouth."

Austin pulled it back and shouted, "My snow machine will make globs of snow, hills of snow, mountains of snow!"

Cheers and applause filled the cafetorium. Kids whistled. They stomped their feet on the floor.

Wendy put her hands around her mouth and shouted, "But wait, here's the greatest part. We could donate all the free tickets for the new water park to the kids at the Circleville Homeless Shelter."

The cheering stopped. "Give up our tickets?" a kid in the front row shouted.

"But we can really have a snowman contest with that snow-machine snow."

Mrs. Stuard pointed to the screen behind her. "Circleville Elementary could have a part in something wonderful. We could put smiles on the faces of kids who don't have much to smile about."

Wendy watched the kids watching her. She held her breath. It wasn't easy to give up free tickets to the coolest looking water park ever.

She raised her hand. "I say that we donate the tickets."

Dennis raised his hand. Then Jessica. Austin raised both hands.

Slowly, the other kids and their teachers' hands shot up until the cafetorium was a sea of raised hands.

CHAPTER 11

Snow Party

Wendy spread out blue folders, white paper, scissors, glue, and black markers on the table near the playground slide. All around her snow covered the ground. The kids at Circleville were building snow forts, snow people, and even snow animals!

Wendy stood a poster board sign at the back of her table. It said: MAKE A SNOW FOLDER!

Several kids stopped by her table.

"What do we do?" a girl asked.

Wendy gave each of the kids a folder. "Fold this paper and cut out snowflake patterns. Then you can glue them to the front of your folder. And I have copies of snow facts and myths to go inside them."

While they worked on making their snowflakes, Wendy waved to Dennis. His table of snow experiments was set up under the big oak tree. There was a big crowd watching him do something with a jar of snow.

Wendy shivered in the cold air. If the day had been more than 28 degrees, the snow would have melted too fast.

"We need more snow over here!" someone shouted.

Austin and his father moved the snow machine toward an area that was almost clear of snow. The pretend snow shot into the air. Wendy laughed when a clump of it landed on her nose.

"Smile!" Jessica shouted as she pointed her camera at Wendy. "Great shot!"

Before the snow party ended, Wendy wanted to play at the snow wall, where several kids were hiding. They popped up like jack-in-the-boxes to throw snowballs at the kids hiding behind the other wall a few feet away.

Mr. Andrews stood beside a game he had built. Kids threw Ping-Pong balls at snowmen made of Styrofoam to try and knock them over.

Mrs. Stuard walked across the playground, her red coat almost white from all the snowballs thrown at her. With a laugh, she knelt down, picked up a handful of snow, and threw it at the kids hiding behind the snow wall.

"We have the coolest principal," Jessica said.

Wendy agreed. And she had the coolest friends.

Mrs. Stuard walked over to them. "I think the party is a big success," she said, wiping snow out of her hair.

"Thanks to Austin," Wendy said. She never thought she would say that about him. But Austin had saved the day. And since he was an honorary Weather Warrior, they all were a part of Circleville being the snowiest school around.

"I got a thank you note from the head of the homeless shelter," Mrs. Stuard said. "He's sending a plaque to our school in honor of our donation."

"Wow," Wendy said. "I can't wait to tell the rest of the Weather Warriors."

"Tell us what?" Dennis asked. He stood beside Mrs. Stuard, eating a lime green snow cone and shivering.

Wendy told him about the plaque from the homeless shelter.

"Hey, let's go tell Austin," he said.

Mrs. Stuard said she would stand at Wendy's table and help the kids put their folders together.

Wendy, Dennis, and Jessica ran across the playground. "Hey Austin, we have some news," Dennis said.

Austin turned and aimed the snow machine at them. They stopped. Wendy folded her arms. "Don't you dare."

Austin grinned and turned the pipe up, shooting the snow so it fell over their heads.

They told him about the note from the homeless shelter and the plaque.

"And Mrs. Stuard says the Weather Warriors can be proud most of all," Wendy said.

Austin stopped blowing the snow into the air. "You mean the real Wendy's Weather Warriors?"

Wendy nodded. "Yep. All four of us."

She scooped up a handful of snow and patted it into a ball. She walked slowly toward Austin. Dennis and Jessica followed her with their own snowballs.

"And now, it's time for your official initiation, Austin Scott," Wendy said.

Austin turned to run as three snowballs flew into the air.

Did You Know?

❄ Snow is a mineral, just like diamonds and salt.

❄ At the center of almost every snow crystal is a tiny speck of dust, which can be anything from volcanic ash to a particle from outer space.

❄ According to Guinness World Records, the largest snowflake ever recorded was 15 inches (38 cm). It fell in Fort Keogh, Montana, in 1887.

❄ In 1885, "Snowflake" Bentley took the first photographs of snow crystals by attaching a bellows camera to a microscope. He captured more than 5,000 crystals.

❄ Winter storms get their energy from the clash of two air masses. The point where two air masses meet is called a front.

Snow Myths

MYTH: When a snowflake melts and refreezes, it has the same shape as it did before!

FACT: This is a tall tale. Water does not have a memory.

MYTH: A ring around the moon means rain or snow is coming.

FACT: It just means that the air is humid. It could mean rain or snow, but not always.

MYTH: Wear your pajamas backward if you want a snow day.

FACT: A fun and silly old idea.

DENNIS'S Favorite Experiments

EXAMINING SNOWFLAKES

You can look at snowflakes. Put the fabric or paper in the freezer for a couple of hours when it is snowing. Take it out of the freezer and put it outside during the snowfall. Make sure snowflakes land on the paper or fabric. With a magnifying glass, you will be able to see the beautiful shapes of the snowflakes.

YOU NEED:

- Black paper or black fabric
- A magnifying glass

MEASURING SNOW

Snow stacks up fast! An inch of snow looks a lot different than an inch of rain. Let's measure snow.

YOU NEED:

- A clear plastic container
- A ruler
- Snow

Fill the container with fresh snow and use the ruler to measure how much snow you have. Bring the container inside and let the snow melt. Now, measure how much water is in the container.

On average, every ten inches of snow equals one inch of water.

IS SNOW CLEAN ENOUGH TO EAT?

Scoop a cup of snow and melt it in the microwave. Put it in a glass. Fill the other glass with tap water. Which looks cleaner? Try filtering the snow through a coffee filter and see what is left behind.

YOU NEED:

- A cup for scooping
- Two identical clear glasses
- A coffee filter